The
Christmas
TALE OF
PETER
RABBIT

William was nowhere to be seen.

# THE *Christmas* TALE OF PETER RABBIT

BY

*Emma Thompson*

ILLUSTRATED BY

*Eleanor Taylor*

FREDERICK WARNE

FOR BENJAMIN BUNNY

TRUSTED FRIEND

DOUGHTY COMPANION

*-E.T.*

FREDERICK WARNE
Published by the Penguin Group
Penguin Books Ltd, 80 Strand, London WC2R 0RL, England
Penguin Group (USA) Inc., 375 Hudson Street, New York, New York 10014, USA
Penguin Group (Canada), 90 Eglinton Avenue East, Suite 700, Toronto, Ontario, Canada M4P 2Y3
(a division of Pearson Penguin Canada Inc.)
Penguin Ireland, 25 St Stephen's Green, Dublin 2, Ireland
(a division of Penguin Books Ltd)
Penguin Group (Australia), 707 Collins Street, Melbourne, Victoria 3008, Australia
(a division of Pearson Australia Group Pty Ltd)
Penguin Books India Pvt Ltd, 11 Community Centre, Panchsheel Park, New Delhi – 110 017, India
Penguin Group (NZ), 67 Apollo Drive, Rosedale, Auckland 0632, New Zealand
(a division of Pearson New Zealand Ltd)
Penguin Books (South Africa) (Pty) Ltd, Block D, Rosebank Office Park,
181 Jan Smuts Avenue, Parktown North, Gauteng 2193, South Africa

Penguin Books Ltd, Registered Offices: 80 Strand, London WC2R 0RL, England

www.peterrabbit.com

First published by Frederick Warne 2013
ISBN 978-0-7232-7694-4
10 9 8 7 6 5 4 3 2 1

Photograph of Emma Thompson by kind permission of Nick Haddow
Photograph of William by kind permission of Yew Tree Farm



Printed and bound in China

# *Dear Reader,*

Imagine my surprise when, during the tenth year of this brand-new century, a celebrated centenarian with very long ears requested that I pen him a brand-new tale.

Imagine my delight when two years later, and owing to an undiminished enthusiasm for adventure, Mr. Rabbit requested yet another!

Wild confidence (possibly misplaced) drove me north to the Lakes, where I explored his birthplace and the many homes and hideouts of his Creator, Miss Potter. At Yew Tree Farm I made the acquaintance of a most unusual person, whose strength of character and peculiar quirks of nature so impressed themselves upon me that he now appears in the pages which follow: he as eager as I to divert and entertain you . . .

Humbly I beg leave to remain your faithful servant.

RABBITS are always very uppity during the Christmas season, and Peter Rabbit was no exception.

AFTER upsetting a third bowl of mincemeat onto the sandy floor, he was sent to his aunt's to fetch a cup of suet.

On the way, Peter bumped into his cousin, Benjamin Bunny. He was looking equally gloomy.

His mother had sent him to Mrs. Rabbit's for a handful of raisins.

"LET'S *stay out of the way for a bit,"* suggested Peter.

*"Good idea,"* said Benjamin.

The cousins set about playing rabbit cricket with holly-berries and fir cones when William sauntered by.

WILLIAM was a turkey.

HE was a puffed-up person, full of his own importance.

Nothing made him happier than his bold, brave fan of tail-feathers which rattled upon the cobbles as he strutted about.

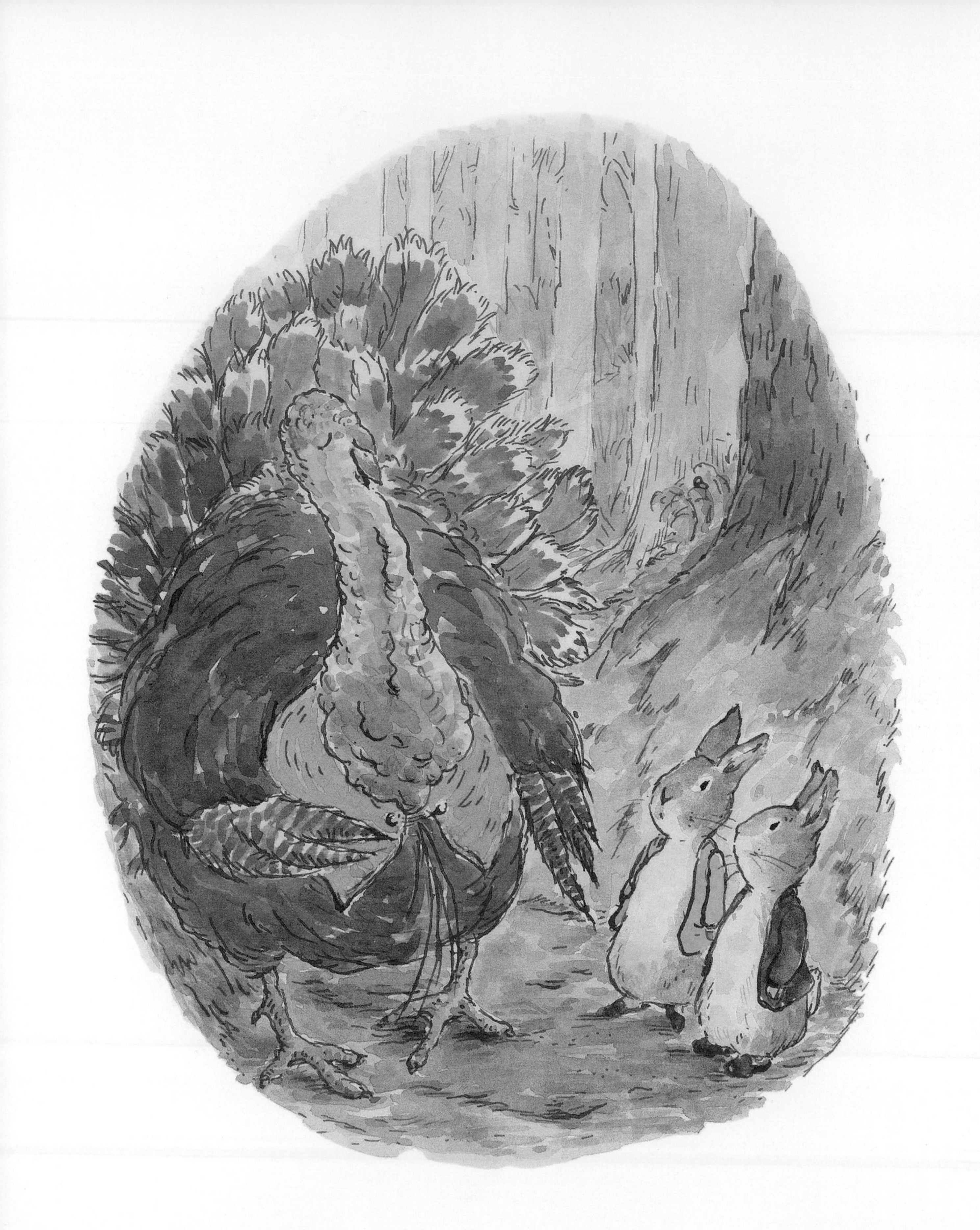

"CHRISTMAS *is a fine time, a fine time!*" he gobbled at Peter and Benjamin.

*"I am not sent to fetch suet or raisins! Mrs. McGregor brings me such treats EVERY day! Nothing is too good! I am their honoured guest . . ."*

and here William lowered his voice and said in an important whisper,

*". . . for they say that on Christmas Day they are to have me for dinner!"*

QUITE QUICKLY, Peter and Benjamin were struck by the
same
horrible
thought.

"WILL YOU TELL HIM – *or shall I?*" whispered Benjamin nervously.

"ROASTED?" said William. *"Are you quite MAD? To think they would harm a single feather on my exquisite head! Never!"*

And he puffed out his chest even more and rushed about in little cross circles.

But then, Peter told him that his father had been put into a pie and eaten by Mr. and Mrs. McGregor.

WILLIAM's wattle went white.

*"Roasted?"* he said again, very faintly.

Peter and Benjamin felt very uncomfortable.

LATER, in a corner of the sandy burrow, the cousins held a whispered council-of-war.

*"We shan't let them do it!"* said Peter.

*"How are we going to stop them?"* asked Benjamin.

*"We'll hide him,"* resolved Peter.

*"Good idea,"* said Benjamin admiringly.

They had both been severely scolded for forgetting the suet and raisins.

THE next day, William was exceedingly relieved to hear of the plan. He had not slept well owing to some very bad dreams.

FIRST of all, Peter and Benjamin tried hiding William upside-down in the shed where the pheasant and woodcock were hung.

THEN they tried hiding him under one of the rhubarb-forcers by the compost-heap.

THEN they tried to hide him in the coal-scuttle.

BUT his fan of tail-feathers always gave him away.

William refused point-blank to fold them in.

Privately, Peter thought him a little too proud for his own good.

CHRISTMAS EVE came and there was a fall of heavy snow.

*"My magnificence cannot be hidden,"* said William mournfully. *"If I run away, they will see my tracks in the snow. I can only wait for the axe to fall."*

Just then, Mrs. McGregor crossed the yard wearing a large bonnet trimmed with feathers. She was on her way to the Christmas Fair.

Benjamin had quite an unexpected idea.

Moments later, Mr. McGregor came into the yard waving a cleaver.

"*Time to dispatch that turkey,*" he muttered, licking his lips.

BUT William was not in his shed.

NOR was he by the kitchen-window waiting to be fed scraps.

HE WAS not even in the vegetable-patch!

IN FACT,
William
was nowhere
to be seen.

WHEN Mrs. McGregor came home to find their Christmas dinner had vanished, she gave Mr. McGregor a frightful row.

*"How in the world could anyone mislay a turkey that size?"* she shrieked.

Neither of them noticed the fabulous new *hat* on the hall-stand.

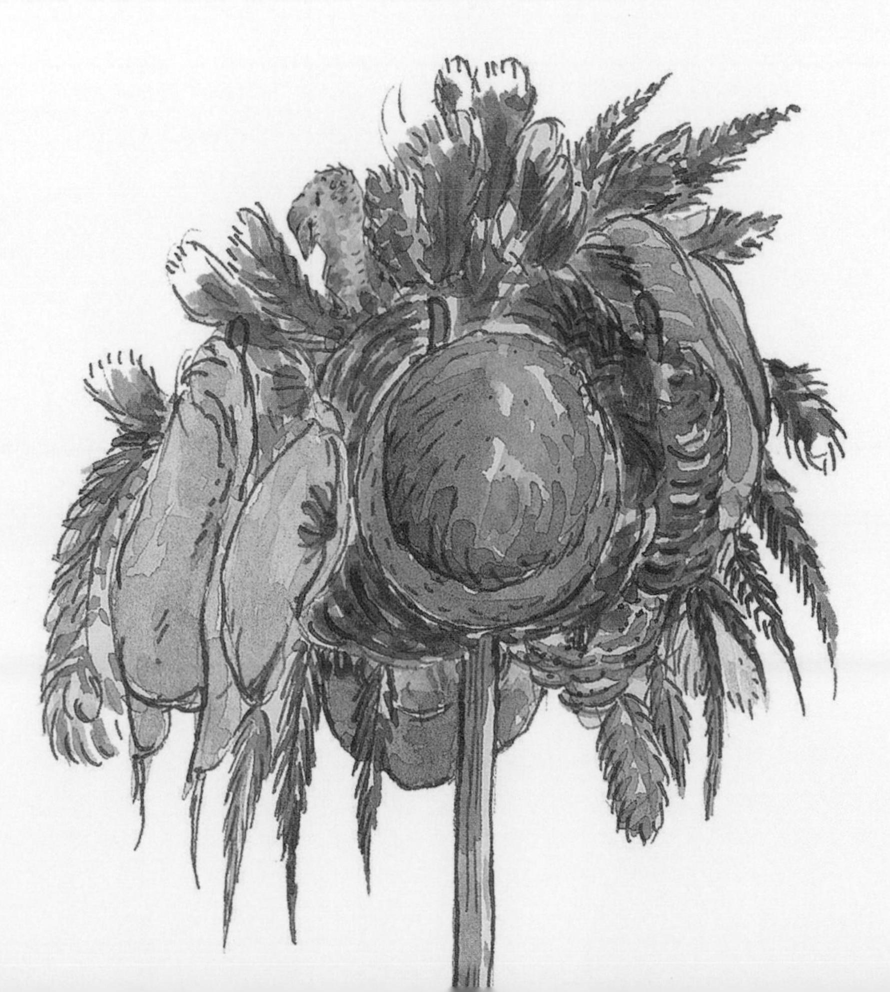

ON Christmas Day, Mr. and Mrs. McGregor had nothing for dinner but boiled potatoes and winter cabbage (the sprouts having succumbed to an early frost).

I AM pleased to say that the Rabbit family celebrated with pickled radishes, lavender wine, mince pies, and a squat black pudding from Cousin Finlay.

William was cordially invited but he was too big to fit in the burrow. Humbly, he offered to fold away his tail-feathers.

But he was still too large so he simply stuck his head in.

LATER, Peter and Benjamin brought out a plate of special barley-cake that Mrs. Rabbit had made for him.

*"Happy Christmas, William,"* they said.

William thought it was the finest thing he had ever tasted.

AT BEDTIME, Peter gave Benjamin a small pat on his back.

*"It was your good idea that saved William,"* he said. *"Well done."*

Benjamin Bunny thought he had never been so happy.

THE END

William, the inspiration for our feathered protagonist, resides with his mate, Kate, at Yew Tree Farm, Coniston. They have recently become proud parents.

To visit him, go to: yewtree-farm.com